For Leo

First published in Great Britain in 2005 by
Frances Lincoln Children's Books, 4 Torriano Mews, Torriano Avenue, London NW5 2RZ
www.franceslincoln.com

Distributed in the USA by Publishers Group West

British Library Cataloguing in Publication Data
available on request.

ISBN 1-84507-289-8

Printed in Singapore
1 3 5 7 9 8 6 4 2

**Visit M.P. Robertson's website
at www.mprobertson.com**

Hieronymus Betts

and his Unusual Pets

M.P. Robertson

FRANCES LINCOLN CHILDREN'S BOOKS

Hieronymus Betts has unusual pets.

KEEP DOGS
ON
LEAD

Slurp the slugapotamus   is his slimiest pet

but Hieronymus knows of something even

slimier!

Screech the greater-spotted howler bird
is his noisiest pet

but Hieronymus knows of something even

noisier!

Gobbler the sabre-toothed rhino-toad is his greediest pet

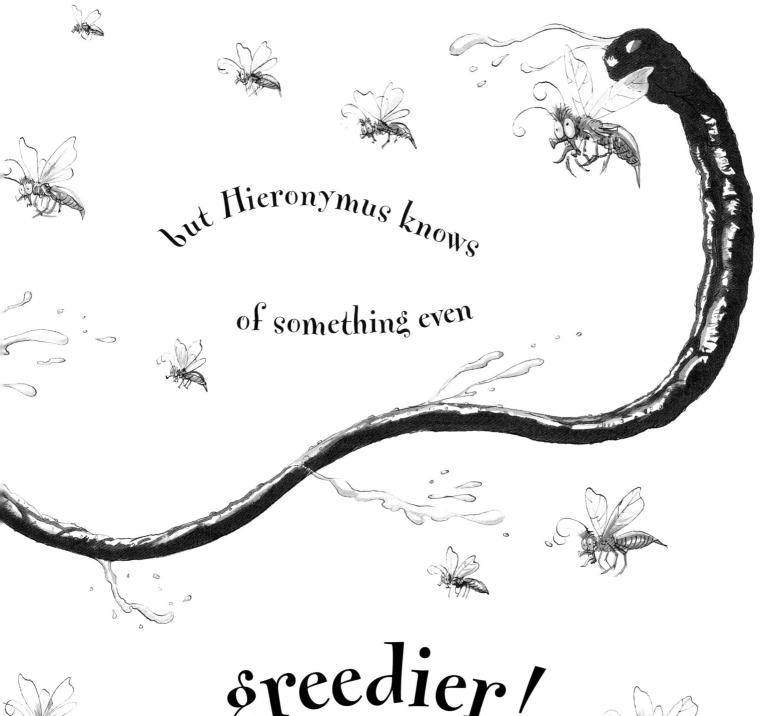

but Hieronymus knows

of something even

greedier!

Cuddles the porcupython

is his scariest pet

but Hieronymus knows
of something even

scarier!

Growler the grizzly hare

is his fiercest pet

but Hieronymus knows of something even

fiercer!

Stinker the bog hog is his smelliest pet

but Hieronymus knows of something even

smellier!

Oojamaflip the whatchamacallit

is his strangest pet

but Hieronymus knows

of something even

stranger!

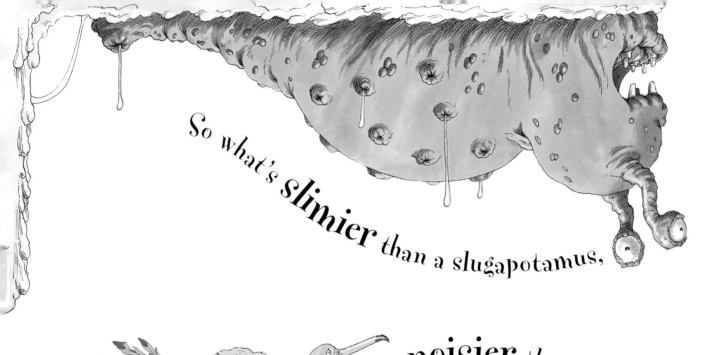

So what's **slimier** than a slugapotamus,

noisier than a greater-spotted howler bird,

greedier than a sabre-toothed rhino-toad,

scarier than a porcupython,

fiercer than
a grizzly hare,

smellier than a bog hog,

and **stranger** than
a whatchamacallit?

Dare you turn
this page to find out?

Hieronymus's
little brother –
that's what!

But even though he's

slimier than

a slugapotamus,

noisier than

a greater-spotted

howler bird,

greedier than

a sabre-toothed

rhino-toad,

scarier than a porcupython,

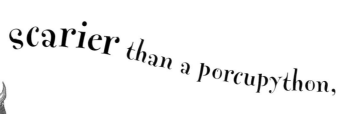

fiercer than

a grizzly hare,

smellier than a bog hog,

and stranger

than a whatchamacallit...

he's more fun
than any pet could ever be!